THIS CANDLEWICK BOOK BELONGS TO:

_____

_____

_____

For Aunt Dee and Uncle Paul
and their delightful tribe
J. H.

To Amelia,
with thanks
I. B.

Text copyright © 2002 by Judy Hindley
Illustrations copyright © 2002 by Ivan Bates

First U.S. paperback edition 2007

Library of Congress Cataloging-in-publication Data is available.
Library of Congress Catalog Card Number 2001025681

ISBN 978-0-7636-1668-7 (hardcover)
ISBN 978-0-7636-3284-7 (paperback)

APS 20 19 18
14 13 12 11

Printed in Humen, Dongguan, China

This book was typeset in Stempel Schneidler and Metropolis.
The illustrations were done in watercolor.

Candlewick Press
99 Dover Street
Somerville, Massachusetts 02144

visit us at www.candlewick.com

Do Like a Duck Does!

Judy Hindley

illustrated by

Ivan Bates

CANDLEWICK PRESS

Five little ducklings, following their mother;

whatever any duck does, so does every other.

So they waddle and they hop
and they scuttle and they stop.

Flop! Flop! Flop! Flop! Flop!

All together.

"Quack!" says Mama Duck,

"That's the way to be!

Do like a duck does!

Do like me!"

There go the ducklings, all in a line.
But who's creep-creeping close, following behind?

"Wait!" says Mama. "You don't belong with us.
Stop!" says Mama. "Do you think you're a duck?"

"But of course!" says the stranger, with a waddle and a strut. "That's just what I am — a big, brown duck."

Well, he has no feathers and he has no beak.
He has four claws on his hairy-scary feet.
He has two ears that stick up a mile,
and a wicked foxy nose
and a wicked
foxy smile.

So Mama says, "Well, then, do like us.
Head up, tail up, toes pointing out.
Stretch your little wings, dear,
straighten up your back.
Do like a duck does.

Quack!
Quack!
Quack!"

Then Mama leads
them off together.

Hup! Hup! Hup!

Five little ducklings and a big brown duck —
a hairy-scary stranger — a very silly duck!

"Look!" says Mama.
"What a lovely patch of muck!
Jump in the puddle, dear.
Show you're a duck!
Lots of bugs and beetles
swimming in the scum.
Open up your beak, dear.

**Yum!
Yum!
Yum!"**

Now the very hairy stranger
has some notions of his own,
and he's looking
at the ducklings
when he says,

**"Yum,
yum!"**

And he's creeping
ever closer . . . and
he's very,
very
near . . .

But Mama turns and catches him,
and says, "Look here!
You don't like bugs.
You don't like muck.
You can't say *quack*. . . .
Are you *sure*
you're a duck?"

"Yes, I am!"
says the stranger.
"It's really, really true!

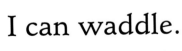

I can waddle.
I can scuttle.
I can strut a little, too.

I'm a duck!
I'm a duck!
I'm a duck like you!"

So Mama says,
"Show it! Prove you're a duck.
Do like a duck does! Do like us!"
Then they zip through the thistles and . . .

. . . they slip into the river. **Plop! Plop! Plop!**

Plop! Plop! All together.

Down go the ducklings, all tails up! And down goes

the stranger. **Glup! Glup! Glup!**

So where are all the ducklings now?
Here they all come.

Pop!

Pop! Pop! Pop! Pop! Every one.

But where's the
very hairy-scary stranger?

Gone home.

"Well," says Mama.
"What a bit of luck.

But I really always knew . . .
that was no duck!"

Judy Hindley was brought up in California, the eldest of six children who all delighted in stories, books, and jokes. She has written more than fifty books for children, including *The Big Red Bus*, *Baby Talk: A Book of First Words and Phrases*, and *Eyes, Nose, Fingers, and Toes*, which the *Boston Globe* called "a first-rate choice for story hours."

Ivan Bates debuted as an illustrator with his art for Sam McBratney's *The Dark at the Top of the Stairs*. He is also the illustrator of *Grandma Elephant's in Charge* by Martin Jenkins, and *Just You and Me* by Sam McBratney. *Do Like a Duck Does!*, Ivan Bates's first collaboration with Judy Hindley, features some of the animals on the farm where he lives with his wife and young son.